MOBSTERS, MILLIONAIRES AND THE GIRL NEXT DOOR

BY

PAMELA WESTFIELD

© **Copyright 2014 Pamela Westfield**
Ocean Cat Publications

ISBN-13: 978-09911217-1-7

CHAPTER ONE

Susan was having a great start to her summer, but she was out of control in every direction. She had been spending money even more recklessly and watching hopelessly as the balance in her checkbook grew smaller and smaller.

She was nearing the end and was down to one bank account. She thought again about how much the $75,000 that she lost to Robert would really help her out now.

She spoke to a lawyer friend about pursuing him, but he said if any drugs were involved, she should decide to leave the whole fiasco alone. She figured when she got her big money she would go after him with high power attorneys.

She wondered where Robert was lately and who he was scamming now. She searched his name on the internet and saw there was plenty of information on him. He wasn't even using an alias! Someone actually had a blog on him and asked that people who had been bilked by him to come forward and tell their story.

It was unbelievable! He had been going across the country for several years and had a long list of victims. No wonder why he was so good at it! Both men, women, hotels, and large corporations had all been charmed, and then coerced by him. She knew now that there would never be a chance to recoup her loss! He was the biggest nut that she had ever met! How could she have been so gullible? She wished she had researched him like she was doing now when she first met him!

She could really, really use that money! Eventually, she was going to have to get some kind of permanent full-time job. After years of non-stop money flow, it was a reality she was not able to face. She was mad at herself for wasting it all and started calculating all the other stupid moves she had made.

Such a waste! It was hard to remember the highlights and the good times. She now strongly resented even more that the StepWitch existed. The thought of going broke, and her problems with all the men in her life, past and present, really began to stress Susan out.

She thought about Robert again and that made her feel even more edgier with a desire for more dangerous men. Her twisted path led her to hanging out at Sicilian nightclubs.

One evening, her girlfriends dragged her to a new disco in the suburbs. It was actually a popular nightspot with a private Italian Social Club connected to it.

Susan chose to drive the group. They pulled up and she announced to the girls "We're parking ourselves! I don't want anyone in this type of place touching my car." Her girlfriend pointed and read her the sign in front of them "Mandatory Valet." Too bad Susan!"

Susan was then surrounded and forced to park by some very greasy men. It was a well known fact at these clubs that if it says mandatory, and you try to park on your own, that there was a good chance that they would either call a tow truck, would steal it, or you would find it vandalized when you returned.

The girls walked inside ready for action! The music nearly blasted them back out as they entered. It was very techno and even had the flashing colored disco balls on the ceiling. The lights contrasted with the Coliseum look of the place. There were several Italian marble columns and small religious statues atop fountains in the corners. The wall was padded with black plush carpeting and red vinyl. Susan felt like she had stepped back into a bad Roman nightmare.

Something else did not fit in with the décor. There were

several tables filled with men only. Many were clothed in old brown coats and fedoras. As they looked further, there was also a grouping of five tables with very snappy looking, well-groomed men wearing Armani and smoking cigars. All were laughing loudly. Their gold chains and diamond pinkie rings flashed in the dark. The girls zigged towards *those* tables.

As they came closer the strong, permeating aroma of exotic cologne lured them even deeper into the men's lair and the girls took a table just a few spots away.

Susan viewed the dance floor. It was almost all women dancing with each other. They were mostly overweight, too much eye make-up, and garishly dressed. She felt like she was at the wedding reception in "The Godfather".

She noticed that the men became quieter, put down their cigars, and were now undressing her table of friends with their eyes. The girls shifted restlessly in their chairs. They weren't sure how they were going to welcome this attention. They could smell the testosterone in the air.

A waitress walked up to one of the men and he made a gesture toward their table. Like an obedient dog, she came up to the girls and asked them what drinks they would like to order. She said "They are on the house!" She smiled in the direction of their provider. He was short, good looking, with a classic bouffant. He seemed to be most interested in Susan and summoned her with his finger.

She slowly rose and with her best slink, she made it over to him, precariously balanced on her five inch stilettos. One of the men quickly abandoned his chair for her and she sat down next to this generous stranger.

He grabbed the leg of her chair and pulled it so close to him that she was almost on his lap. He said something in Sicilian to the other men and they nodded their heads. Three of them went up to her girlfriends and walked them out to dance.

In a sexy, heavy Italian accent he said "I was telling them that you were the most beautiful girl in the world. My name is Dino and this is my place." He then introduced her to his friends remaining at the table.

The men seemed like they had been in a heavy discussion and were not completely pleased by this interruption. They politely smiled at her and continued talking with each other, leaving Dino free for her.

Her drink arrived and Dino placed the cherry from his glass into it. He held it up for her as she sipped. She smiled and looked into his eyes. They were friendly, but she also sensed a menacing feeling about them. He was definitely an "in-charge kind of guy." At the table to the left she noticed two scary men, well-built with no necks. They were dressed in deep black. They were both watching the door and her every move. Dino saw the quizzical look on her face.

"Those are my bodyguards, just ignore them." She laughed, thinking he was kidding. Then she looked again. One man actually had a black gun sitting on the table in front of him.

Susan felt a hollow tremble inside of her resounding into a feeling of sexual desire. Dino put his arm around her and she was ready for the taking. It was magic and it was trouble. She knew he was someone that she could not turn down. And she definitely knew she was a little tipsy to think sensibly.

When Dino began kissing her the other men moved to another table and the bodyguards looked away. She noticed her friends were watching her from the dance floor and shaking their heads "No" at her.

They felt intimidated by their partners and were afraid to quit dancing. They gave her a pleading look like they wanted to get out of there.

Dino's soft touch now became more aggressive and he was all over her, rubbing her legs and not so subtly fondling her. She thought he was going to jump her right there. He whispered "Let's get out of here."

They stood up. Amused, she noticed he was inches shorter than her, even without her heels. One of his bodyguards grabbed her purse and the other one got her coat. Dino hurried her out the front door.

She looked back over her shoulder and could see her girlfriends looking at her like they should come to her rescue. But their partners pulled them further into the middle of the floor obstructing their view.

A black Town car was waiting. Dino helped her into the back seat and they drove only a few blocks to a small hotel. His driver got out of the car and walked into the office.

Susan could see through the window that the desk clerk looked very nervous. It looked like the driver was demanding the key to a room and no money was being exchanged. He came back to the car, opened the back door for them and slipped the key into Dino's hand.

Dino pulled her into his arms and ushered her out of the car. They walked a short distance and into the small room. She noticed that his bodyguards were now present again and seated in a black sedan. The Lincoln driver had slowly followed Dino and was now parked directly outside the door.

She was disappointed. The lighting was bad and cast a dim yellowish tint to the walls. It was very seedy looking, a four hour nap kind of place. Even worse, it was more like a half-hour set-up! She could smell mildew on the aged furniture.

Dino threw her on the bedspread like a cave man. She was reaching for her shoes when he grabbed her ankles, pulled her to the foot of the bed, and said "Baby, leave those spikes on! Oh, God are they hot!"

Then he plowed into her! She didn't know if she could handle him. He was built like a stallion!

A short time later there was a knock on the door. She heard an Italian voice say "Let's go." She tried to collect herself. Dino walked ahead of her to the car and gave her a quick kiss on the cheek and nuzzled her neck. "You were a good girl. Now go with them."

His two bodyguards pulled up. Dino shoved a business card in her hand. "Call me! I've got to do some stuff now." She was given a ride back to the club as the bodyguards sat silently in the front seat. They pulled up on the street, not even at the entrance, and rudely said "OK, go."

She now felt very cheap and was mad that she had been with Dino so easily. His bodyguards made her feel like she was just a whore. Susan noticed that her friends were now standing in the lobby door. "Let's get out of this place" they said nervously. One of her friends stared at her. "What happened to you?" She did not need to answer. It was obvious. She felt damaged and still weak.

She might be acting wild lately, but she felt she was still too classy to have a man treat her like he did. Back in her normal days, *whenever they were*, she was usually very conservative and did not sleep around. "Never again," she said to herself. "What a jerk!"

One of her girlfriends asked her "Do you want to go somewhere else?" Susan replied "No, I just want to go home." She drove off in her car and her friends took a cab to continue club hopping. She took a long warm bath and went to bed.

Susan had only been asleep for an hour when the phone rang. Reaching down she started pulling the cord out of the wall. She wondered, "Who the hell is it?" She held up the phone and heard "Hello darling, did you miss me?" It was *him*. Bewildered and reluctant to talk, she said "How did you get my number?" He replied "Your girlfriend gave it to my friend." "Oh, great, "I'm changing this number tomorrow" she thought to herself.

Dino started angrily speaking Sicilian to someone in the background. She thought she heard a woman's voice. Still groggy she said "What do you want?" He said "I love you. I must see you again tonight!" She then heard the voice again. It definitely was a woman. "I've got to go" he said, and hung up.

Now she was wide awake. Mad that she couldn't fall back asleep, she went out to the living room and watched television. She was very confused. About forty-five minutes later, she heard a soft horn beeping outside. She ignored it at first, and then parted the curtains a few inches and looked out.

The two black cars were there under the streetlight. Then the phone rang. She was nervous and felt required to pick it up. She said nothing and heard "Darling, come down here. I need you!" She peeked out the window again. Dino was standing on the grass with one of his arms stretched in the air toward her. She said nothing and quietly hung up the receiver.

Two minutes later there was a strong knock at the door. It was his bodyguard. "He wants you outside." He hesitated and then said "Now!" "I have to get dressed" she said very flustered. "I'll wait" he stood in the doorway, his body filling the frame. The other bodyguard came up. The first "Neck" said "Tell him she's coming."

She dashed to her bedroom and locked the door. She at first wondered if she should call the police. Then she threw on some tight jeans, kitten heels, and an even tighter silk shirt. With no time to add make-up, she slowly opened the door.

Like a prisoner, the two hulks led her outside with her standing between them. This no longer seemed exciting for her. She was worried about what Mafia nightmare she now had gotten herself into.

Dino walked up to her and kissed her. She did not return any affection. "I'm very tired. What do you want?" "You're coming with me now" He replied, mad at her reaction to him. Sullenly, she sat down in his car. Dino yelled "What's the matter with you? What's the matter?" His accent was thickening the madder he got. She felt daring. "Who was the woman?" His eyes widened and glaring "What woman?" He looked puzzled and then said "Oh, on the phone. That was my wife, forget about it." He gave her a chilling look.

She instantly shut up and he put his hand on her knee and began gently cuddling her. "Come on baby, I'm crazy about you!" She looked out the window. It was that very silent part of the night. Dawn was still far away. This was the time of night when bad things happened, when no one could hear you scream.

He buried his head into her chest like a baby. She felt distant for another minute and then he nosed in some more, looking up at her winking. She now felt more relaxed and started patting his head. He had a great head of hair that was stiff with gel and still perfectly styled. "Hey, hey, easy on the hair, I need to look beautiful" he said.

She started liking him again and reached down kissing him behind his ear. She noticed they were driving in the direction of his nightclub. It was still lit up brightly and in full swing.

They walked into the lobby and went up a side staircase, with the bodyguards following behind. They went through a wide door as the men took their places on each side and stood guard. The upstairs was set up like a VIP room. There was a private bartender and just a few tables. Six older men were seated at one of them. Dino walked her over to a couch and gave her a kiss. "Here honey, you stay over here. I have to talk business with these guys. I just wanted to have you with me tonight and to keep you near me."

Dino and the men were deep in conversation. They were speaking Sicilian and it sounded serious. Susan knew some Italian and could understand snippets of what they said. The men seemed nervous about her presence and kept stopping to stare at her. She ignored them. She slunk down in the couch cushions and easily dozed off.

When she woke up, Dino was sleeping on the other side of the couch. The room was very bright now. It must have been late morning. The door was open and no bodyguards were present. She tried tapping him on the shoulder, but he only turned over.

She looked around the room and then out the window. His Lincoln was parked in front. "I'm going home" she said. She began rocking him "Can I get a ride?" Dino mumbled, "Sure, sure just tell the driver. I'll call you later." With his eyes still closed, he smacked his lips and blew her a kiss.

She made her way down the stairs and outside. She thought "Why did he even bother getting her? They didn't even do anything." She tapped on the driver's window. He was busy talking on his cell phone and ignored her. She went to the back door, got in, and was driven to her place.

As their relationship progressed, Susan was never sure if she wanted to be a part of it. She could tell Dino was seeing more than a few other women, and it didn't really bother her. She just wished he'd fall for one and leave her alone. The more he sensed her dissatisfaction with him, the more possessive he became whenever her feelings started wandering off.

When Dino brought her to the club with him he often would leave her sitting alone at a table. Plenty of his friends were ready to jump her, but, they never did. In addition to "Omerta", the second rule was never mess with the "Goomah" of the boss.

Carlo, one of her favorite admirers, was there one night. He was very handsome. He was watching her and she smiled at him. Dino was upstairs in his office. She stood up to go the restroom.

As she walked down the hall she sensed someone was behind her. It was Carlo! He grabbed her shoulders, shoved her against the wall, and started sucking on her neck. He then swung her into the ladies room and locked the door. Kissing her savagely, he pulled his gun out of his waistband.

He laid her out halfway on the sink counter and pushed her up against the mirror. "Oohlah" was all Susan could muster in between heavy breaths. She laughed "Carlo, get off of me. What are you doing?"

Carlo rasped "You need Carlo, don't you?" "You'll want me forever now and I'm going to give it to you whenever I see you!" She was trying to pull herself together and said "You know I am dating Dino. I don't want you. What are you? Crazy?"

"Screw Dino, Screw Dino, I'm gonna kill that guy, I'm gonna whack him!" His phone started buzzing. The voice on the other end was speaking loudly "Get out of there Carlo! Dino is back downstairs!" Carlo lifted Susan off the sink. "I will see you later baby!" He then swaggered out the door.

She straightened up, cautiously opened the door and looked both ways down the hall. She also looked up at the ceiling to see if any cameras had caught the action. There was one mounted there but it was facing the other direction, so she scurried down the hall.

Susan arrived back at her table. Carlo was still gone from his. She tried to collect herself and ordered a glass of wine. She was busy looking down and fumbling in her purse, so she didn't pay any attention when the drink arrived.

A hand placed it on the table before her. She looked up. It was Dino! She became very nervous and started fidgeting with her feet. He sat down next to her pulling in closer. "Oh God, he's going to know," she could feel her already red cheeks growing crimson and started to sweat.

"What's the matter with you, you look so flushed?" He took her wine glass and rubbed it against her face. "You weren't dancing without me, where you?" She then saw beyond his shoulder that Carlo had come back and was sitting at his table again watching them. Now she started to tremble. "What do you do when I leave you for so long?" Dino scolded, "How come you never come up and visit me?" He turned his back on her and stared a hole right through his nemesis. Carlo gave him a defiant look and talked to his friends out of the side of his mouth. He then reached for his cigar which had been left in the ashtray from his earlier hurried departure.

A very young waitress, probably not even legal age, came up to Carlo offering him a light. He started puffing to get it going, never once taking his eyes off Dino. Carlo then very deliberately put his arm around the waitress.

Susan didn't know that Dino had a thing going with the waitress, but Carlo did. Dino saw them and whirled around angry and grabbed Susan a little roughly. "Let's go." She protested "Where?" He growled, "Let's get some dinner." She noticed Carlo was still flirting with the girl and was rubbing her back as he watched them leave.

One of the bodyguards walked up to Dino and he whispered something to him. The bodyguard nodded his head toward Carlo. Dino then waved both of the bodyguards off. They went outside. Dino walked down the block in silence with Susan until they reached a small Italian café.

As they were seated at the table, she could see that Dino was preoccupied with something. He kept polite talk with her but wasn't acting normal. "Could he know?" she thought. He was such a poker-face with his emotions she couldn't figure out anything with him. He was taking long gulps of his drink in between the awkward pauses of their conversation.

After an especially long stretch of silence, he blurted out "What's wrong with you!" She wanted to crawl under the table. "I know what you're doing!" She looked scared. "You're playing me! You don't think I notice?" He started swearing at her in Sicilian. She wouldn't respond and was studying him.

Even though she was innocent, she couldn't see how he knew about Carlo, so she waited for him to offer more information before pleading guilty to anything. She giggled at him. "What are you doing with yourself when you're *noticing* me?"

Dino whined "No, come on, be serious, what are you doing to me?" She asked "What is wrong with you?" He said "Just don't play me, don't do it, I don't want to hurt you." He threw some money on the table for the bill. "I've got to go!" He rushed out of the café leaving her at the table. She was amused and quite pleased with herself "What was that?" She loved the fact that he was unnerved, maybe this meant he truly liked her. She was going to definitely see how far she could take this and how much she could financially get out of him. She needed some guilt-free spending money.

Susan knew she no longer actually liked Dino. She just wanted to mess with him. This new vulnerability he was showing had really turned her off. She was going to have her fun with him and then end it.

As she walked back down the street from the café, Carlo came speeding up in his Lincoln. He pulled up to her, leaned over, and opened the door for her to get in. "I am ready to try for that other round beautiful!" She giggled and sat next to him. Too bad she *was* with Dino. Carlo was much hotter and taller!

Carlo got right to work. He whispered "You're mine now! I am going to make you feel real good!" He pushed the button to recline the seat and then pushed himself on her. Susan wanted him too and felt like she might surrender this time.

Lights flashed in their eyes and a dark car pulled up quickly blocking the Lincoln at the front right corner of it. A woman jumped out of the car and ran over to Susan's door. She flung it open. "You Bitch! Get out of there, you are a whore!" She grabbed Susan and pulled on her until she dropped out hard on the pavement. Susan was petrified!

The woman then dove in the door and started hitting Carlo. He grabbed her hands and pulled her into the car laughing at her. "Calm down honey, calm down! I'm not doing anything! We're just talking, she's Dino's girl. I was just giving her a ride back to the club to meet him." She looked at him like she didn't believe him.

He got out of the car and helped Susan off the ground. "Are you alright? You can get back in, everything is fine."

Susan said "Who the hell is that? Your wife?" He answered "No, no, it's just one of my girlfriends. My wife would never be that stupid! Come on. Let me drive you to the club." Susan said "No way!" She walked away from him quickly.

The woman got back in her car and followed his car to "God knows where!" Susan had just seen her life flash before her eyes. That woman could have easily had a gun, and in that brief encounter, it would have been curtains for her!

Susan now swore, with the exception of Dino, that she would never knowingly mess around with a married man ever again. She couldn't believe she had been so callous and selfish in her thoughts about this before.

She pulled out her cell phone and hurriedly dialed her girlfriend. "Hey, come and pick me up. "I'm free tonight, let's go downtown."

They had a great time and did a lot of dancing and flirting. Susan had a strange feeling that she *was* being watched. Now that Dino had planted that in her head, she was feeling very uneasy about it. She knew it wouldn't take much to get him to sniff her out and then snuff her. He could make things happen.

It was totally laughable whenever the press said the mob no longer existed in Chicago. It was just that no one knew where the secrets were buried. They weren't as open these days when they whacked someone, but it still happened. And everyone that needed to know, did.

As the weeks wore on, Susan contributed as little as possible to her relationship with Dino. She showed less interest in having sex and he didn't push it. He seemed more interested in focusing on his club and hanging out there.

He had now opened a casino in the basement that was only open to his crew and closest buddies. He had several slot and poker machines down there, two craps tables and even a small stage for select comedians and Sinatra wannabees. She usually chose to remain upstairs in the disco area. Tonight, there was not much going on up there, so she went downstairs. She saw a few men playing the slots. She didn't see Dino and walked into his private room where the door was half ajar.

He was sitting at his desk with a big pile of money in front of him. Seated on his lap was the young waitress with her cleavage pulled out of her uniform. Dino, with cigar in hand, looked like he was ready to do a "Bill Clinton" when he saw her.

Susan screamed "You JERK! You're worried about me all the time! What the hell is this?" He was caught off guard and struggled to reply. He whispered something in the girl's ear. She bounced off his lap, adjusted herself, and walked like she didn't care, out the door. He now looked at Susan. "Oh, come on baby, it's nothing, you know that" he said and stuck his cigar in his mouth.

Dino thought he could easily dismiss the confrontation by virtually ignoring her. He started counting his money. She drew her arm back and took a big swat at the pile, knocking it all over the desk and floor.

She then reached down, took a big handful of it and then ran upstairs screaming "I deserve this Dino for all the crap I have taken from you!" He did not follow her. The waitress was outside in the hall. She watched Susan leave and then came back in his room while he closed the door.

Once she was back in the disco, Susan sat down and tried to stuff the bills into her purse. She must have grabbed around five thousand in hundreds. Luckily, she didn't grab the dollar bills. She was feeling very freaked out and was afraid Dino was going to come up after her. Some of his friends looked at her from their table and were quite amused. They were shaking their heads. It was obvious that she had just had a fight with him.

Susan wasn't afraid enough to leave. She wanted a drink and she didn't wait for a waitress. After all, Dino was probably doing all of them! She went straight up to the bartender and demanded her own bottle of Absolut and a shot glass. She then went back to her chair and pounded them down. One of his friends laughed and had a waitress deliver a carton of orange juice to her, not even in a pitcher.

Susan looked so mad! His friends just watched her and felt sorry for Dino, and what she was going to do to him once she was successfully loaded. She sat there by herself for a half-hour. She noticed Carlo come in the door and he had a date with him. This made her even madder.

No one approached her. No one asked her to dance. So she went outside carrying the bottle with her and sat on the curb. She saw Dino come out of the basement entrance by himself. His driver pulled up about a hundred feet from her. Dino got into the car and did not even notice Susan. As he drove off, she threw the bottle at the car, just bouncing it off the tire.

For the next month, whenever Susan saw Dino's number on her caller I.D. she would hang up the phone. She began going out every night to Rush Street with or without her girlfriends, and danced all night, building up quite a presence. At the best clubs, she would always pounce her way into the VIP section and have her pick. Although, she didn't hook up with them, there were also

Hollywood celebrities that flew into town that she got to know.

They would often keep company with her because she was easy to talk to and she knew to just act normal and not gush all over them. Chicago was a much easier place to have access to the stars than other places. They came out because they were probably bored at their hotels and they didn't have to usually worry about paparazzi here.

One night, she was at one of the retro bars. Susan was making her way to the dance floor, when a well-dressed, slim-built man came up to her. "I noticed you have long fingers. Can I see your feet?" She thought it was a funny request, so she pulled off her shoe.

He reached down, held one, and looked like he was getting excited. She grabbed him to dance; she liked his weirdness, and stayed with him until the bar closed.

He told her he was a movie producer from Hollywood and invited her back to his hotel just to party, nothing else. She said she was not interested, so he gave her a big hug and said good bye. She had to pull back because his cologne was so overpowering. She could taste it in her mouth!

As she was walking back into the bar she looked at her cell phone and noticed that Dino had called an hour ago, but did not leave a message. Even though it was late, she knew he wanted her to call back and she was wondering why he would still talk to her. She was afraid that it was about the money she took from him.

She decided to start driving towards his nightclub before trying him. When she got about ten minutes away she dialed him. One of his waitresses answered. "What are you doing with Dino's phone?" Susan demanded. "Who the hell is this" the girl replied even surlier and said

"His phone was sitting on the bar."

Dino came up on her and grabbed the cell. He saw it was Susan's number. "Hello, trouble-maker, how are you beautiful?" "Hello Dino!" Susan was glad that he was happy to talk to her, and a bit relieved.

He said "Where are you Honey? Come and see me tonight! I want you!" Susan questioned "Are you sure you want to see me? You're not mad at me?" He laughed "You bet I'm mad at you. What where you doing that night? I miss you Honey! Get over here!"

Susan agreed to drive over. "I'll see you in my office" he told her. "Which one?" she asked. "Upstairs, or in the basement?" "Basement. I've got to keep my eye on the slot action. I've got a couple of guys down there now making too much money off me."

Susan was not sure if she trusted him to meet him down there and thought it was suspicious that he did not seem angrier at her. After all, she did grab a lot of money and had already spent it. She had no intention of paying it back.

When she got to the club, there was no valet. So, she left her car parked in front of the Social Club entrance and went in. Not even a bouncer in the lobby. "Pretty strange" she thought.

She went down the narrow basement stairs. There were only two men at the slot machines and no one at the card tables. The dealer was sitting in a kitchen chair in the corner with his head down on his chest sleeping.

Dino's office door was half open. She saw a man sitting in a wooden chair with his arms tied behind him. One of Dino's bodyguards had a leather blackjack and was hitting him in the knees. Dino was sitting down on a large couch which was a new addition to the room since she last saw him. He was casually smoking a cigarette. "Come in, come in" he gestured.

She looked around and walked in, keeping her cell phone close in her hand. The bodyguard untied and pulled the man out of his chair, taking him down the hall. He looked at Susan with a pleading look in his eyes. She heard a door slam.

Dino said sweetly "Sit, sit" patting the cushion next to him. She sat down with hesitation and he put his cigarette out. He immediately tried pulling her into his arms and she inched back from him, she was afraid that he would smell the Producer's cologne on her, it was that strong! She abruptly stood up. "I have to go to the restroom to freshen up first." Safe in there, she tried washing off the scent, but it was too pungent. She was afraid to return to him.

She slowly walked back. Dino wasn't in the office. She went out to the bar area and fixed herself a drink. Sipping it as she walked back in, she noticed the gamblers had left and so had the sleeping bartender. The room where the man had been taken was now empty.

Susan went in and closed the office door. She turned on his TV and sat on his chair to wait for him. A short while later she heard someone lightly knocking on the door. "It's open Dino" she called. Another knock. She laughed "Dino! Get back in here!"

The door opened wide and an enormous man with dark hair and a very deep tan was standing there in a T-shirt and a pair of red gym shorts. His neck, arm and leg muscles looked like they should be on an Olympic weightlifter. He also had a prominent bulge in his shorts that was stretching them tightly forward. He looked like a freaking gorilla.

Susan was completely surprised and didn't know what to say at first. She just stared at him. Right when she was saying "Who are you?" Dino's top bodyguard, who Susan hated, but was now relieved to see, peered in from the side of the giant and said "The boss wants you to take care of him." She yelled "What are you talking about?" He sternly said "He wants you to make him feel welcome. He's fresh off the plane from Sicily. His name is Rico."

Susan was ready to throw her cell phone at him. "Are you kidding me?" She figured it was a big joke and that Dino would show up next laughing. "No, seriously, he wants you to do it with him!"

The hulk repeated him in broken English "Do it with me." The bodyguard told him "Show her what Dino gave you." Rico's shorts were now almost ripping in front with how hard he was. He smiled at Susan and pulled out a very tiny condom from his top pocket.

Dino now came to the door and said to her "What's the matter? Do him, he needs it, he likes you! At least give him a blow job!" He then started speaking in Sicilian to the monster. His bodyguard left laughing.

Dino then walked fully into the office pulling the gorilla's arm. "Come on Susan, you're a little whore. Show him how much!" "Come on, you slut, here I'll pay you." He walked towards her "I know you've been messing with Carlo and everyone else!" He reached over to his desk drawer to get some money.

Susan started screaming "What are you talking about? Let me out of here!" She pushed by both of them to make her escape. She ran out into the bar area. "Dino you pig, this is it, I'm going to make it so we are really through!" She grabbed her cell phone and pushed one of the speed dial buttons. It was for Dino's home. Susan waved it at him. "I'm calling your wife Dino! It's over asshole!"

Dino started to rush towards her tripping on the stairs as he tried to go up them. Susan ran ahead, trying to keep her balance while holding the phone up, out of his reach.

She heard a woman answer on the other end. Susan screamed into the phone "Dino is a crazy Bastard and he cheats on you all the time!" She kept running as she heard his wife swear and slammed the phone. Dino yelled "I am going to kill you!"

Susan pushed the upper door at the top of the stairs closed and threw a chair at it. She ran even faster outside to her car. She fumbled to click her key chain to open the door, pushed the panic button instead, and the car began beeping. Dino was now right on her heels. She slammed her knee on the wheel as she threw her body inside. She started the car as Dino reached her door handle.

The car started to move. Dino now came in front of it. She was so scared that she veered and jammed her foot on the brake. Somehow, Dino doubled over and rolled off the hood. Susan swore she saw him reach to his side for his gun.

She managed to tear off, driving over the club's front lawn, through the bushes, and almost into a tree. She kept the accelerator pedal dangerously to the floor for several more miles. She knew she could not go to her house. She really did it this time! Dino was going to be out to get her! He was not the one to mess with.

CHAPTER 2

Susan had refused to see Lt. Murray for at least two weeks after that night and was now thinking of going home to Illinois. While she determining what course to take, they still continued at a lukewarm pace.

There was something about Doug that she just wasn't ready to give up on yet. She was surprised he never apologized, maybe he didn't remember that night since he was drunk and on pain pills. She was always able to find an excuse for things. No wonder why she continued to find the wrong men.

Susan was more than ready to date civilians again. She had heard about a fun Oldies event that was held every week-end outside the city. It was always packed! Susan grabbed a friend and they drove over there to see what it was like.

It looked like a lot of men from New Jersey spent time there. Lots of nice Italian boys. Some were dressed like they were straight out of the 50's with their hair slicked back and their tight jeans rolled into a cuff.

Susan was asked to dance right away and was having a great time. Her friend was getting close to one man that kept her sequestered at a table with him holding hands. In between songs, Susan went over to her friend to tell her that she was going outside for a moment.

As she walked, she heard a very thick New York, or maybe Jersey accent "Hey! Where ya going? You aren't leaving, are you?" Susan turned around. There was a man about her height with thick dark hair and looking a lot like an Elvis during his good years. Susan laughed "Elvis? Is that you? You really are alive!" "Ha, Ha, very funny" the Elvis answered.

He reached into his leather jacket and pulled out a pair of the famous big rimmed tinted glasses." He put them on and dramatically posed. Now he did look exactly like him! He said "I *am* Elvis, I am the Tollbooth Elvis. Haven't you ever seen me on the road?"

Susan apologized "I'm not from here, I'm usually in Chicago." She held out her hand "Pleased to meet you. Are you leaving now?" Elvis said "No, I came out looking for you. Here come over to my car. I want to show you something." Susan walked through the lot with him. He pointed to his black Mercury Grand Marquis. She was a bit disappointed he didn't have money, he was only driving the "Poor Man's Lincoln." But, he was a character so she was glad to talk to him.

They jumped in his car. He turned up an Elvis song and reached for his glove compartment. Susan saw a gun, and was relieved when he only pulled out his driver license. "Here, look at this, he smiled." It showed him dressed as Elvis in his white leather jumpsuit, and it listed his name as Elvis Presley with his address at Graceland. He seemed very proud of it. Susan thought this was pretty juvenile and now he was starting to bore her.

He put it back and when he was reaching over this time, he put his hand on Susan's knee. She had no problem with this move and felt no allegiance to Doug. They started kissing and then were grabbing at each other. He sat back and said "I'm taking you over to my house. We're going to make love. You've never had it from Elvis before. Right?" He started driving and Susan had no clue where they were going since she was not familiar with too many areas.

They pulled up to a dark house on a street where the

cars where parked up on each other's bumpers. There was a group of kids standing on the sidewalk trying to look tough and smoking cigarettes. Elvis waved at them.

He took Susan's hand and brought her to a side door. They went down a short staircase and into the basement. He turned on the light to reveal a nicely furnished room with tons of Elvis memorabilia everywhere. He even had a life size dummy of Elvis clothed in a black studded leather jumpsuit. Over his single bed was a flag of Elvis. "I guess you like The King!" Susan joked and she sat down on his couch.

He walked off to his bathroom and came back in a black sweat suit. Susan always liked the way well-packaged men looked in sweats. He was definitely doing his Italian heritage proud. He stood in front of her and then eased down and started giving her a lap dance.

"This is something different" she struggled to say as he was crushed against her chest. "I don't like germs" he said. "I don't know where you've been."

Susan was insulted and annoyed he was acting like this. He then tried to have sex with her still wearing them and it was really turning her on. She was dying to have him in her. "Please" she said. "Take them off!" He gave in. Pulling them down he laughed, "Oh, OK. Here comes Elvis..."

He went right to work forcing her against the side of couch. She had one leg on the floor and he held the other one up with his hand. He pounded her for a long time and kept gyrating to satisfy every area. She could hardly keep up with her breathing. They peaked as she thrusted her hips up at him. It was fantastic! He looked down at her and said "That's why they really call me Elvis, The Pelvis!"

Then he made himself look like a jerk when he abruptly said "OK, let's go, I don't want my mother to see you. She'll be home soon." Susan looked at him with doubt "You live with your mother?" Elvis acted mad "I live down here, I don't live with her!"

"OK, OK" Susan said. She decided she better not try to ask him more. She looked around and noticed he had no kitchen. In addition to Elvis stuff, he also had posters from Grease and football pennants on the wall. His Italian mother obviously did all his cooking and probably his laundry too. He was the perfect Mama's Boy. Susan wondered if her name was Gladys.

They drove back and his body language was a complete reversal. He acted just like a shy boy that had just lost his virginity and not like a man his age. He pulled back up to the dance hall's front entrance. Susan asked "Aren't you coming back in?" He said "Naw, I am going back home. Here, you can have this." He handed her a glossy photo of himself and the directions to his toll booth assignment for the following week. I'll be in Lane 2 or 3, he smiled at her.

Susan felt he was acting nice now and he was one of the best lays she had ever had. She nodded "Maybe I will come and see you. I can bring you some Starbucks." Elvis grinned. He said "Hey, give me your number. I almost forgot." She got out of the car and reached into her purse, scribbling her number on a scrap of paper "Here you go Your Majesty! That was quite a performance tonight. I enjoyed it!" He waved as he did a backward U-turn and drove away.

Susan's friend was standing inside the lobby. She said "That guy was married that I was sitting with. Why didn't you come back sooner?" Susan laughed "At least he didn't live with his mother."Her friend informed her "Welcome to New York! All the men here have some kind of mother issues." Susan told her "I am definitely ready to get back to Chicago. I think I've run my course here."

A couple of days passed and Susan thought more about leaving New York. She had just started pulling boxes out of the closet, when her phone rang. It was Elvis! He had the day off and wanted to come and stop by in the next hour. Susan knew what he really wanted, and she was game!

Right after she clicked off, the phone rang again. It was Doug. "I want to start treating you better and actually take you on a real date." His offering was hard to get tickets for a dinner show that night featuring Rat Pack imitators. Susan liked Sinatra, but this era was still way out of her age range. She pretended to be excited, was a bit apprehensive, but accepted his offer. She told Doug to call her when he was about ten minutes away.

Susan cleaned up her apartment as fast as she could. She wanted to hide her boxes, but Elvis showed up sooner. She let him in and he lunged at her and cornered her. He was wearing leather pants and looked hot! They made out for several minutes. He was a lot more romantic than Doug, not on meds, and obviously a lot better in bed.

He held her hand and walked her over to the window. He pointed below to the street. He said proudly "That's my 1962 Mercedes 190SL convertible!" Susan leaned out. It was cherry red and amazing! She said "Let's go for a ride! Elvis said "We can do that later. For now, I'm going to ride you!"

He grabbed her hand and walked her into her bedroom. Susan warned him "You really need to take it down the block to that pay parking lot. They have security there. This neighborhood isn't the greatest." Elvis said "I don't want to pay for parking. It will be fine down there. I'll keep my eye on it."

Susan said "That might be a big mistake, you should move it. I'll come with you and we can drive around!" Susan did want to badly check it out, but as soon as he laid her down and started kissing her again, she forgot all about it. They made love the entire afternoon and she was starting to regret that she had to be leaving soon for her date.

They were about to start into it again when there was a knock on her door. Susan looked at her clock. It was already 5:30 PM. She thought it must be her landlord and she chose to ignore him. She jumped back on Elvis, when the knocking became very loud. "What the hell?" Susan walked out of her room naked and stood by the front door.

She asked in an angry voice "Who is it?" A rough voice answered "It's me! It's the police! It's time for our date." Susan felt panicked. "Doug?" Doug was mad now "Who the hell else do you think it is?" Susan complained "It's too early! You were supposed to call first." Doug replied "We need to get a jump on traffic. We are going into the city."

Susan didn't know what to say. She could hear Elvis moving around in the bedroom. He leaned out her door and said "Who is that? What's going on?" Susan tried to shush him. She knew the front door wasn't locked and that Doug would probably turn the knob any second. She was trying to keep her arm on the door and convince Elvis to get back in the room at the same time. She whispered at him with a hiss "Get back in the room!" Elvis started to protest.

Doug started talking louder "Is someone in there with you? I'm going to shoot through this door if you don't open up!" Susan turned the lock on the door as quietly as possible. "No, I'm just getting ready" she said. "Doug, I've got to wait for my landlord to come by. Can you go to the bar at the end of the block? I will meet you over there in a half-hour."

Doug looked through her peephole, and of course could not see in. He moved his fingers and tried to see if he could screw it off. "Are you sure no one is in there? Don't jerk me around!" Susan was exasperated "Doug, come on, I'm not ready. I'll meet you at the bar. OK?" Doug said "I guess that will be alright. Hurry up, will you? We have to get going!" Susan assured him "I'll be there."

She listened by the door to hear his footsteps creak down the hall. She then looked out the window to make sure he was getting in his car. She was worried that Doug was going to hang around and watch for her, and she knew that he would shoot Elvis if he saw her with him. He considered Susan a possession and could treat her any way he wanted. Susan kept watching as his car drove off.

She was about to turn back in from the window when she was startled. The convertible was not there! "Oh my God!" Susan yelled. Elvis said from the bedroom "What? What's the matter?" She pointed, "Your car is gone!"

Elvis screamed like a girl "Are you kidding?" He ran to the window. "I can't believe it! This cannot happen!" He ran into the bedroom and grabbed his pants, his jacket, and his cell. He hopped while he was putting them on and ran outside without his shirt or shoes. It was quite comical.

Susan could only think about the fact that she had to get over to meet Doug. She only had time to worry about herself. She was ticked this was all happening and that she had no time to shower.

She started to slide herself into a little black dress and went looking for her pearls and earrings in her jewelry box. She looked great and was definitely ready for Manhattan. She put on her black Louboutins with the silver-lined heels and ran to the elevator.

When she got downstairs, Elvis was in her lobby and on the phone with the police. He cupped the phone and turned to Susan "I can't believe it! Some asshole stole it in the middle of the day. My wife is going to kill me!"

Susan said "You're wife? You're married?" Elvis ignored her and finished talking to the cops. He hung up. "Yeah, my wife! It's her damn car and I don't know what I am going to tell her!"

She was angry with him for being such a liar and a cheap idiot, and especially for leaving such a valuable car on the street. "I don't have time to talk about this! Here's your shoes and shirt! I've got a date."

Elvis said "A date? Was that him at the door?" He started digging into her. Susan cut him off "I have to leave! You don't live that far from here, so maybe the cops will drive you home. You're married! I don't care! Just go! Bye!" Elvis watched with his mouth open as Susan drove off in her car.

Susan couldn't handle any more stress and as she headed to the bar, she thought about Elvis. She really liked him! She had even considered staying in New York to see where they were headed with each other, but she was also afraid of what Doug would do if she broke up with him.

She thought more about Elvis and his basement shrine. That was where his wife probably sent him when she didn't want to be around him. Then, she guessed that they all probably lived there with his mother and that she cooked them all their meals. Who knows? Maybe there were little Elvises...She screamed to herself "Who cares?"

She saw Doug's car outside when she pulled up to the bar. She parked in front of it and went in. He was sitting at a table drinking a beer. Very strange, Doug did not mention anything about went on earlier. He just smiled at her and said "You look beautiful. Are you ready to go?" He looked very good in an expensive suit.

The traffic was awful as they drove into Manhattan. Doug pulled the car in front of a large restaurant. He reached into the glove compartment, grabbed his extra gun and put it in his pocket. He then let the valet take the car. It was very windy and cold for September and she pulled her coat closer as they walked in.

Susan was very impressed with the place. It looked like it was filled with New York's elite. She looked at Doug and thought how handsome he looked and that she was proud to be there with him. She felt bad that he might think he was screwing around with him earlier.

The waiters started serving dinner and half-way through it, the lights dimmed and the show started. The actors did a decent job looking like the Rat Pack. With the exception of a really bad wig on the Dean Martin impersonator, they were pretty convincing. But, it wasn't her thing.

She started fantasizing about Elvis and she could feel her cheeks getting hot. Doug interrupted her thoughts "Are you enjoying the show?" Susan lied "Sure, it's great. Thanks for bringing me." Doug thought he knew what she was thinking "Don't worry. It will be over in a minute. Do you want to go dancing somewhere?" Susan said "I'm kind of tired, I wouldn't mind going home."

The show finished up ten minutes later. As the audience clapped, Susan gathered up her things and sat poised to leave. Doug left to get her coat and Susan looked down at her cell to see if Elvis had called. He had sent her five texts and left three voice mails.

Susan looked around the room and watched as the tables were ending their evening. She saw a familiar figure that was standing behind his date's chair and helping her up.

It was Michael Hansen! Susan felt her heart go into her throat and she started to tremble. At the same moment Michael noticed her too and quickly made his way over, leaving his girlfriend at the table with an astonished look on her face. It was clear she was floored by such a blatant abandonment.

Michael practically pulled Susan from her chair and gave her a bear hug and a big kiss on the cheek. "Susan, I am so glad to see you! What are you doing here in New York?" He didn't give her a chance to answer and then hugged her even harder as she managed a little squeak "Michael, it is so great to see you too!"

They both looked at each other and it was apparent that they would have both started into each other madly, if Susan hadn't regained her composure. Susan said "Michael, I am on a date with a cop and he might shoot you if he sees me talking to you." Michael laughed "Aww, come on you're kidding..." Then he suddenly shut up.

Doug had returned and the expression on his face soured when he saw that Susan was talking to another man. Michael looked at him and said "Wow, I better get out of here! Where do you find these loons? I really need to talk to you Susan! Can't you give me your number? Just say it quickly! I'll remember it. Please, I seriously need to speak to you!"

But, there was no time. Doug walked back to her as Michael scooted away. All the niceness that Doug had displayed earlier was long gone. He growled "Who the hell was that pretty boy?" He pulled Susan roughly from her chair. Susan answered coldly "I know him from Illinois. He's a neighborhood friend. Don't worry about it! What's the problem?"

Doug just stared and was ready to confront him, but then snapped back and decided against it. He smiled at Susan, taking her hand gently and said "Please don't react like that Susan, I was hoping we might get tighter than we have been. I want to spend the night with you. Are you ready to go?"

Doug turned and walked in front of her. Susan looked behind her and noticed Michael was now reasoning with his date. It looked like he was having a very difficult moment. Susan laughed to herself.

During the ride home to her house, Doug chattered away about sports and Susan sat quietly. She was now thinking fondly about Michael. She also began wondering if Elvis was still stranded in her lobby, or if he had managed to get a ride to his house.

They pulled in front of her building and Susan was very nervous that she would see Elvis standing there. Doug remained seated and took her hand. He smiled "Are you sure you don't want to stay out? Don't you want to go dancing?" It was very creepy that he was acting so nice to her and she really didn't trust this new personality on him. It was how movie murderers acted before they were going to hack someone. Susan thanked him and said "No, I am still calling it a night." Doug said "I'll call you." Susan answered "That will be nice. Good bye." She was relieved to see her lobby empty and went up to her apartment.

Susan kept herself busy the next day completely mystified that Doug had been so nice to her the night before. She decided that Elvis had been pretty desperate to contact her, so she called his cell. Elvis answered "Is that you Susan? Wait a minute. I am at work. I've got to close my booth."

He took a minute activating the gate to close so no more cars could come through. He then turned off the lane's green light overhead. He came back to the phone "Boy, that was so screwed up yesterday!" Susan was concerned "Did you get the car back?" Elvis said "No, no word about it and my wife won't even talk to me today. I can't believe you ditched me like you did! Susan said smugly "What did you expect? You deserved it! You should have told me that you were married so I wouldn't have wasted my time!"

Elvis replied sarcastically "Whatever! How was your dream date? What bar did you pick him up in?" Susan said honestly "He's a cop I've been dating for a while and he is really getting on my nerves. I am ready to dump him." She added "You are much better in bed!"

Elvis liked that she said this. "Susan, I would like to see you some more. Can we still do that? You don't really care that I'm married do you?" Susan forgot about her new hands off husbands policy and said "As long as she doesn't shoot me in the back. She's Italian too, isn't she?"

Elvis said "She'll never know. She didn't even figure out why I had her car in your neighborhood. She was too freaked out to do any heavy thinking. She's not that bright, anyway. Kind of boring."

Susan said "We know I am never boring." He said seriously "I want to see you after work today. Do you want to do that?" Susan agreed "OK, call me before you're

35

going to leave." Elvis said good-bye.

She was very glad that Tollbooth Elvis was still in her life and looked forward to seeing him. A few hours later he knocked on her door and gave her a bag with a cold hamburger and some fries in it. "Well, at least you brought me something" she laughed.

He sat on the couch, turning on the TV. She sat down next to him. He was still wearing his tollway uniform and looked pretty corny. Hard to picture him as a sexy beast in it. She didn't think she liked him all that much after all.

Susan waited for him to make a play at her and nothing happened. He was absorbed in his television show. She watched him ignore her for a half-hour and then angrily said "What's wrong with you? Are you having second thoughts about your wife? And what about your mother? Does she live with you?

Elvis looked mad and yelled "What the hell does that matter?" Susan grabbed his arm and said "You can't yell in here. I think it's time for you to go!"

Elvis stood up and said "Yeah, that's right! I shouldn't be here. I don't think I should keep this up because it will never go anywhere. I don't want to be with you and the cop too. You might give me something!" He walked out the door.

Susan chuckled "So much for that! She was glad she never told Elvis that she would be rich soon or he would have dumped his wife in a second and then she would be stuck with him! What a tool!" She walked into her kitchen to look for her cell phone. She thought about calling Doug. At least hanging with him was *something* to do.

She finally did hook up with the lieutenant later that evening and they had a lackluster time at her apartment. After that, she saw him a handful of times through the month. She would still meet him after work at the cop bar, but was always finding new excuses not to finish off with him at his place.

One night he called her late sounding very drunk, and said she needed to come over right away. She was very apprehensive about going there. He was waiting for her at the door looking very red-eyed.

Susan said "Hello Doug. What's up?" He took her hand and mysteriously led her upstairs to his attic and switched on the light. A little siren went off. She looked ahead and saw a collection of police awards and memorabilia adorning the place.

There was also a black bulletin board which featured a few pictures of dead men lying on morgue carts with their eyes staring open. Susan felt sick seeing them and turned away. Doug announced proudly "This is my Wall of Honor!"

He reached into his top shirt pocket and slowly pulled out another photo, "Umm, fresh kill." He then pushed it on the board with a thumbtack.

Susan didn't want to know who the picture was of, or who was responsible, she could only guess. Doug's pupils were very black. He was obviously heavily medicated this time and looked like he was existing in a far-off place. He also seemed nervous and probably now regretted letting her into the room.

She looked closer and noticed there were three more thumbtacks. He knew what she was thinking and laughed, "I figure by the time I retire, I will have the complete set." Susan thought she was going to become ill.

Doug kept on with his morbid story. "You really need to come by the precinct during Christmas. The homicide guys always have a great tree with the pictures of this year's murder victims on the ornaments."

Susan could not figure out why he would bother her with all of this and she sensed he was going to get nasty with her again. She didn't want to end up on the board or even up against it. Doug looked depressed and walked off to the adjacent bathroom.

That was it! This was too much and Susan just wanted to get out of there! She gathered her purse and ran down the attic steps. She could hear him coming out of the bathroom as she reached the first floor.

Running to her car, like the devil was chasing her, she looked back and could see his silhouette in the front door watching her.

Susan thought over the next days how weirded out Doug was becoming. She wondered if she should tell someone what she saw in his attic. Her girlfriends back home would have thought she was "certifiable" to be dating a guy like this.

She now devoted herself to hitting the town and enjoying it as much as she could. One late night, as she entered her apartment, she could see the red light on her answering machine blinking against the shadows. She was afraid to push the button to listen to it. She walked past it a few times and then pressed it.

"Susan, Susan..." It sounded like a nursery rhyme. "Where are you? It's 3 AM slut! Why aren't you home? Death to your kitties..." Then a click.

Susan shook her head like she was exorcising a bad demon. "What the heck is he saying? I don't even have cats!" That was the last time she heard from Doug. She kept away from all of the cop bars for the rest of that month.

Susan decided that Doug, Elvis, and especially Dino

could screw themselves. They were all losers! She wanted to go back home, she was now definitely done with New York. What she most desperately desired was to go back to Palm Beach and pursue classier men, but she still could not afford to live there yet. Dangerous men, rich men, they all had a common underlying thread and always wanted to be in control.

She called up a few of her friends to see if Dino had ever tried to ask them where she had gone. They all reported back that they hadn't heard a peep out of him. One of her male friends told her that he saw Dino at a club downtown cuddling up with one of his ex-waitresses. Susan thought all along that he probably cared less and she wished she had never left. She planned to stay one more month and drive before the snow storms came.

She enjoyed the rest of her stay without any boyfriend or dating complications. She limited herself to just flirting and was surprised how less stressful it was. She made it into the middle of the next month and was thinking of staying longer.

That was until she began to receive a series of phone hang-ups late at night for the last few days. She had an ominous feeling and decided to get out of there before Doug became spooky and came after her. She decided to leave the next morning.

She wanted to enjoy the city one more time before she left. It was early and she knew some friends were already out. Their cell phones went to voice mail, so she went to look for them. She walked into an Uptown bar that they usually frequented and learned she had just missed them.

She was ready to go out the door when she saw Officer Joe. He had gotten off his shift early. She was glad to see him, but held up her hand like a warning, "I don't want to hear about Doug! Please don't say anything!" He complied.

After a drink, he started talking about Doug anyway and of course, Susan had a keen interest. "You know Doug is back with his ex-wife, don't you?" Susan couldn't believe it! She said, "I thought she threw him out for good!" Officer Joe said, "No, it turns out he was buttering her up all summer in order to get her to lessen up on her child support from him." Susan gave him angry look. "That pig was cheating on me with her?"

She thought back about the few weeks when he wouldn't call her. One of those times she had driven by his house and noticed the newspapers were piling up on his sidewalk. Susan knew she was such a narcissist to assume he would never stray from her. She added casually "I guess it's good he's back with her, at least for their daughter. What a psycho! I have no doubt she'll soon dump him for good, I hope she takes him for everything!"

Officer Joe was amused, "I think he's looking to stay with her. He said he wished they never divorced." Annoyed, Susan ended the conversation, "Well, it was good to see you Joe. At least I had the chance to say good-bye. I am going back to Chicago tomorrow." Joe gave her a kiss and said "We'll see you when you come back!"

****

A few months later Susan was sitting at her desk at a boutique advertising firm where she was the permanent Operations Manager. She was proud that she had kept the job this long. The only reason she liked it and could tolerate sitting at a desk was because she was usually the only one in the office. The others were always out in the field and she had no one to bother her.

She was surprised when her cell phone rang. She thought she had turned it off. One of her sisters was calling her to let her know that the StepWitch had been recently admitted to an assisted care facility and had passed away. She seemed sad about it and said she was flying out to the funeral.

Susan politely said she was not able to leave town and to extend her condolences. Her sister knew it was pointless that she even asked her to come. As Susan hung up, she jumped up in the air "Ding Dong, that witch is dead!" Finally! Margaret had been so awful to her that Susan could not muster up any human feelings towards her, even after all this time.

She immediately called the Trust Vice-President of the major bank that was handling her father's money. She was well acquainted with him since he had turned down her past attempts to get an early loan against her inheritance because the StepWitch was against it.

Susan was surprised when he actually answered the phone. He told Susan that he was unaware that Margaret had passed away and said he would start the wheels in motion as soon as he confirmed it. He told her that due to the fact that this trust had been around for a while that it would not be difficult to get it set up for the final distribution to Susan and her siblings.

That was such great news! It was unbelievable that she now was going to get a lot of money! Though she had been far from hitting the skids, she would finally know again how it felt to be financially secure for life! It was such a sense of relief.

She had to sit down and slowly absorb it all in. She was glad no one was in the office. She did not want them to know she was getting money and would probably be quitting soon. Forget about the spending of her first inheritance, Susan was now ready to go global! This was going to be fantastic! Even though she now had enough money to more than take care of herself, she felt even stronger that she needed to go find her millionaire husband. Make that a billionaire!

There was another hour before she had to leave work. She started looking on the internet for flights to the Palm Beach airport. She planned on popping down there the next week-end to start looking for a house with a pool. She began strategically thinking. To live on Palm Beach in a decent house, not a condo, would involve over a few million and a ridiculous amount of property taxes each year.

Her cell rang again. It was the Vice-President. He told her that he now found out that it might take a few months or more to close the trust, because it turned out that Margaret's financial advisors had brilliantly manipulated the legal loopholes to defer paying any taxes on the principal's interest that she had collected.

Thus, they would all have to wait until Margaret's own estate was settled before they could finalize her father's holdings and also release the remainder of her mother's money. He said he could issue an immediate check to her for only one hundred thousand.

Susan just wanted to get on with her life. As Susan hung up the phone she yelled to the ceiling and flew up her arms "She is still screwing me over!" She knew that all she could do for now was to rent in Palm Beach again. She picked up her purse, locked the office door, and took off a few minutes early. She couldn't stand to wait until 5 PM. It was too much! She was Palm Beach-bound and was ready to make a big splash! There was no more time to waste!

When Susan got home she called the movers, started packing, and she was off to Palm Beach three days later. She had the bank wire the money to her account...

CHAPTER 3

Now that she was getting older, Susan felt more of a need to do the looking. She had no time to wait for her prince to just show up on her doorstep. She certainly did not envision her future being an old maid with cats, but it could happen, since she was too picky about what she wanted.

She thought about how she handled the situation with Anthony on his jet and determined that she should have never brought the subject up. She should have tried harder to develop the relationship with him and see where it would lead. She hoped she would have another chance with him.

On Saturday afternoon Melanie called and let her know that they had landed. The girls planned to meet up and then follow each other over to the party. Susan spent a few hours dressing and changing her mind. When she finally decided what to wear, she only had a five minutes left before she was supposed to see them.

The girls laughed when Susan walked up. They were all wearing white outfits and looked like their mothers had dressed them alike. Susan groaned and went back home to change while Melanie and Linda went back to the penthouse.

They re-grouped an hour later in front of the country club as they had the valet take their cars. It was one of the older clubs on the island and it was quite a step up to be invited to it. The girls walked in sync like runway models as they strode through the main lobby. Men walking past with their wives and dates couldn't help turning their heads to look at them. The girls were worried that they were the only ones there on their own. As they walked through the banquet room doors they were relieved to see that there were single men everywhere!

Linda giggled "Guess we'll be finding ourselves some

husbands tonight!" She tickled Melanie in the side and almost made her fall off her heels. As Melanie tried to regain her balance, a gorgeous man with short blonde hair reached out his arm to help her.

Susan laughed "I guess she found hers!" The man smiled at Melanie and said with a heavy French accent "Please come sit with me. My group is over there." Melanie began to walk with him and said "Sorry girls. Opportunity is knocking!"

Linda and Susan headed over to the open bar and were quickly joined by a small group of Swedish men vying to get their beverages and their attention. They spent a short time accepting after-dinner dance requests and business cards before they moved on to find Ariel and their table.

They looked over to the right and saw that Melanie was comfortably seated with her Frenchman near the front of the room. Linda said "Lucky girl. Guess she found herself someone in the upper ranks. Hope it works out for her." Susan and Linda sadly looked at each other and both knew what the other was thinking.

They cheered up when three very handsome men walked up to the table. Ariel had obviously arranged to have them seated next to the girls. The man that was handpicked for Melanie stared down at her empty seat and looked puzzled.
Susan looked at the exceptionally dapper gentlemen and thought it was possible that Ariel had paid for them to be their escorts. She was very wise when it came to throwing successful parties.

Escorts on the island were not for sex, they were social and dining necessities for unattached and widowed women in order for them to attend the parties. Susan looked closer at their tuxedos. They were not cheap, but they also were not designer issue. They had that shiny rented look to them. She nudged Linda and whispered.

The girls enjoyed their male company and conversation during the elaborate dinner, but kept their eyes discreetly searching around the room for other choices. If they were truly escorts, then the men would understand.

After dessert, Susan and Linda graciously excused themselves and slowly made their way to the far side of the room. They grabbed Melanie by her arm as they walked past her and pulled her up. Susan said "Sorry Melanie, you are going to have to suffer with the rest of us." The Frenchman stood up to protest her departure. His attempt was futile. Melanie just smiled at him and said good-bye.

The trio found another table near the dance floor and lowered themselves to sit. The Frenchman came right back to Melanie and regained possession. He took her out on the floor for a slow dance. It was not long before Linda was soon scooped up and Susan was left to sit by herself. She looked around at what prospects were left and saw Anthony standing over by the bar area talking to a group of men. She turned her chair slightly to avoid looking straight at him.

He must have just arrived. She thought about inviting a man to dance to save face, but she remained seated and confident. One of Ariel's daughters saw her and sat down next to her. It was obvious that she had a few drinks in her. They talked for a while and then the girl decided to give Susan a short history of all the men in the room. She told her interesting facts about three of them when Susan stopped her and subtly pointed towards Anthony.

"What about that one? Do you know anything about Anthony?" The girl sighed "Oh yes, Anthony. Every girl in Palm Beach wants to know about him. But he is a true enigma and no one can get through to him. I have never seen him with an actual girlfriend. Though, I have heard rumors about some girl that broke his heart in New York. Then I think she got killed somehow. That's all I know. He seems to date a lot, but usually just socially. I have never seen him on many second dates."

Susan looked again at Anthony and felt sad for him. When she was with him in the Bahamas they were so intimate and free with each other that she felt there had been a strong bond between them. She didn't think he was hiding his heart from anyone. Anthony noticed her and gave her a nod and a sad look. Susan returned a small smile. He never came over.

Susan's spirit was no longer at the party. She went back over to sit at Ariel's table and watched Melanie and Linda with their partners from a distance. Susan didn't dance and Anthony didn't either. He just stayed in the same place as different groups of friends approached him. He seemed to be enjoying himself.

The party ended at midnight and Linda and Susan went to the front steps to retrieve their cars. Melanie left with her Parisian. Linda said "We will call you in the morning to go shopping if Melanie ever surfaces. We are not leaving until Monday." Linda studied Susan with a worried look. "Are you going to be alright?" The valet pulled up. Susan said "I'm fine. Thanks for coming." She gave Linda a hug and climbed into her car.

Susan wearily drove home. She walked into her house and sat down at the kitchen table. She opened her small clutch to look for some aspirin and noticed that her phone indicated that a text came in. It was from Anthony. All he had done was type out his phone number and put a question mark after it.

Susan felt better but didn't think she was brave enough to call him back. She said out loud "Can't he make a better attempt than that? Does he really care if he hears from me?" She wondered what prompted him to contact her and where he went after the party.

That night her moments with Anthony vividly played themselves out in her dreams. They were together as long as she did not wake up.

CHAPTER 4

Susan woke up early the next morning and walked down to the beach. It was very windy and the ocean was angrily pounding the shore with its waves.

Susan preferred the wilder days to the tranquil ones. It was raining and it masked the tears that slowly escaped from her eyes. It was the perfect setting to match the turmoil that was going on inside of her.

She knew she should be happy that Anthony sent her a message, but she wouldn't let herself get hopeful and project that they were going to be together again. She had to guard herself and not anticipate anything or it would really do a number on her. She didn't know why she let him make her feel so down. Maybe she just was feeling tired.

She walked for a long time picking up small shells and tossing them back in the water. She put her cell phone down, took off her leather sandals, and began walking out into the water up to her waist. She was too upset to worry about any sharks this time.

She could feel the warmth surround her as the swell came up higher. Her toes dug into the bottom and she felt the sand sift through her toes as it loosened and sunk her deeper. She just wanted to emotionally release herself, and she thought this would revive her.

She took a deep breath and let the next wave submerge her. She kept her eyes tightly closed as the tide then lifted her up and carried her away. She could feel her body being tossed in different directions as the wind changed its mind. She remembered she was near the tunnel and almost wished that it would pull her to its core.

When she opened her eyes she saw that she was an uncomfortable distance from land. She looked sadly towards the horizon and then turned around. Laying back she watched the dark clouds grow blacker as another wave swept into her and washed her up on the shore.

Susan sat on the beach for a long time with her head down as the fog enveloped her. She began feeling cold, so she stood up, shook out her sandals, and made her way back to the street. As she looked up she noticed a black Ferrari was sitting down the block. She couldn't tell if anyone was in it.

Her phone vibrated and then rang. Susan hopefully looked toward the car and then to the phone to see who was calling. It was only Melanie. She said "Well, I feel like sludge because I stayed up all night, but let's go shopping!" Her enthusiasm perked Susan up. "OK, I'll meet you two over at Neiman's in an hour." As she was hanging up, the Ferrari slowly made a U-turn and drove off in the opposite direction. Susan thought it had out of state plates, so she didn't think it was Anthony.

The afternoon lightened up and being with her friends brought Susan out of her melancholy. They decided to get manicures, see a movie, and then hit up the clubs off the island. Melanie didn't mention her friend from France. If she wasn't offering information, Susan knew better than to ask.

After the girls returned to Los Angeles, Susan felt a little lonely through the weeks that followed. Melanie and Linda were two of her favorite friends. Besides Ashley back in Chicago, her other acquaintances never seemed to fill the void. They just all seemed to use each other to get through the week-ends or to have someone around so they weren't alone if they wanted to go out. Some of them she didn't even talk to on the phone unless it was the day before they were supposed to do something.

At times, Susan wondered if it was maybe just her that acted like she was using people. Because she was doing it, maybe that is why she perceived it was going on all around her. Although, she was very out-going, she made it hard for people to know her true personality and what she was feeling. Even in a crowd she sometimes felt alone.

Many of her friends, especially the Palm Beach ones, she couldn't even trust enough to introduce to a new boyfriend. None of them knew about Anthony! Susan always felt that if you really liked a man, that you never let your girlfriends know how wonderful he was, or they would move right in on him. The true friends never did that.

One of her island friends called to tell her about a charity bachelor auction that was taking place that night. She had heard that celebrities were even flying in to participate. Susan was not aware of it because she had not been paying much attention to the social events on the island lately. She thought that it would be a lot of fun and agreed to go.

At 7 PM a limousine pulled in front of her house and Susan climbed in to join her four girlfriends that were dressed to kill. They were passing around a bottle of champagne and enjoying the limo's psychedelic disco effects as the wall panels changed patterns with the music.

The auction was being held in a large restaurant. The attendees sat down to a five course meal before it started. The men for sale were milling about wearing large cards on their suits with their numbers on it. They were doing very well at flirting with their prospective owners and drumming up enthusiasm.

The event finally started with the single members from the Palm Beach Police and Fire department being auctioned off. They were wearing their uniforms and looked very hot! One of Susan's friends laughed and started the bidding at ten thousand.

A half hour later Susan walked out to the lobby to see if

another one of her other friends had arrived yet. She opened the glass door and peered out onto the street. She felt a hand on her shoulder and turned around.

"Susan, I am so glad to see you!" It was Anthony. Susan looked startled. She looked at his coat and noticed he was wearing a number. He poked at his card and laughed "I'm going to be one of the bargains tonight!" Susan felt shy and smiled at him.

Anthony was bubbly and said "So why didn't you call me? Didn't you get that text?" Susan didn't know how to answer him. She felt like she was in a dream that he was talking to her. It had been a while since she had last seen him.

Anthony looked concerned at her silence. "Susan, I need you to do a big favor for me." Curious, she finally spoke. "What would that be?"Anthony pulled his checkbook from inside of his suit coat "I don't have much time until I am up. I want you to buy me. I like this charity and I want to make sure it makes enough money tonight. One of my friends is on the committee and talked me into this."

He pulled out a check and started writing on it. He handed it to Susan. It was made out in her name for $80,000. She loosened up with him now. She held it up laughing "You think you're worth that much?" Anthony gave her a friendly leer "Depends on what you want to do with me."

Susan replied "You mean I will really win you?" Anthony said "Absolutely! You are the only woman that I want to have own me." Susan felt her emotions returning. Anthony was getting ready to walk back in to the room. "Susan, we need to talk about what happened. I don't want to lose you. You need to know I reacted on the jet as I did because I am not used to sharing my life with anyone. I like to keep things private. That includes my business and my feelings. Believe me. It is better for you that way."

He paused and carefully continued. "I saw you in the ocean last month. I have been very worried about you." Susan looked at him. "That was you in the car? How did you know I was down there?" He answered "Susan, I make sure that I know everything about you. You are very important to me." He had no time to keep talking and started to walk.

Susan was a bit puzzled by what he said but cheerfully followed him into the room. She went back to her table and was feeling very happy and relieved. She understood in some part what he meant about being private. She knew even more that she needed him in her life.

One of her friends looked at her "What are you beaming about?" Susan smiled "You'll see."

Anthony now joined the small line of men left that were waiting to go on the stage. He didn't tell her that he was the last one and was the grand prize. His number was finally called and he hopped up the stairs. He looked just like a GQ cover. His dark hair and classy Italian looks made him stand out. He was so debonair!

The bidding resumed and the opening amount was $50,000. Susan worried that she was not going to be able to afford him. She tried to catch his eye to get some sort of sign from him on what to do, but he was too busy charming the audience.

The women in the place were going wild. Susan raised her hand to bid the $80,000, but the price kept rising as the crowd reached a fervent pitch. It was like being in a male stripper club! She wondered if Anthony knew that he was going to be that popular tonight. She thought about bidding much more but didn't want to do that unless he had approved it. She was also thinking of putting her own money into it, but decided not to.

The final bid was $150,000. It was made by a famous

heiress from Germany. She was obviously single and was beautiful! Susan nervously watched as she went up on the stage and pretended to stuff her winning check down the front of his pants.

The crowd had a good laugh as Anthony pulled her hands off him and up over her head. He then kissed her cheek, put his arm around her, and walked her off the stage and into the hallway.

A lady in the audience said loudly "Wow, is she lucky! They really look like they were made for each other! They look like Barbie and Ken dolls!"

Susan remained at her table having a parting drink with her friends. She wasn't sure what her next move should be. A minute later she could feel her phone buzzing in her purse. She saw a text from Anthony. He had inserted smiley faces into it and it read "I will call you tomorrow. I miss you."

Susan was very happy with how he was now acting. Her girlfriend broke the spell when she went over to the banquet table in front of the stage. It had the lists of what the bachelors promised to do for their dates.

Her friend held up Anthony's itinerary and started reading aloud. It was for a date the following day in St. Croix. Anthony would be flying the winner there on his private jet.

Susan's heart sunk. This was more than she could bear. Anthony looked a little too happy when the heiress won him. She now felt like going back to the ocean and swimming away.

She was very quiet on the limousine ride back to her house. Her friend asked "Why were you bidding 80,000 dollars on Anthony Fiore? Do you know him?" Susan shook her shoulders "I've seen him around. I was just doing it for the charity." All the girls laughed in unison "Yeah, right Susan. What aren't you telling us?" One of the girls added

"He's going to have a memorable time with Margit. She's an infamous man-eater." She studied Susan to watch her reaction, but she remained stoic.

Susan arrived home and prepared for bed. She was just about to turn her cell phone off when it rang. Anthony was laughing on the other end "Why didn't you bid more for me? Don't you want me?" Susan answered "I wasn't sure you would want to go that high." He said "How was I to know Margit would bid that much. I'm scared!"

Susan replied "You're a big boy, you will be alright." Anthony said "I am going to tell her I have to sit with the pilot in the cockpit and help him fly!" He begged "Seriously Susan, I am going to send the jet back for you and I want you to meet me there for dinner. I am only obligated for the day in St. Croix, not the night! I don't want this wrecking anything between us. Will you please come and meet me?"

Susan said "No, no that's crazy. You don't want that." Anthony insisted "Yes, I do! I am going to wear a parachute and if she tries anything I swear I will jump out!" She started laughing hard "I'll be sure to rent a boat and rescue you then. You will be fine. I am not going. I have a late luncheon to go to for gala planning."

It seemed that Anthony was satisfied that he did his best trying to convince her. Susan wondered if it was just an act. She wasn't all that worried. They talked for a bit longer and then signed off with Anthony saying "Good night dream girl."

Susan went through the motions the next day but her heart wasn't into what she was doing. She was going to feel uneasy until she saw Anthony again. As each hour passed she kept picturing what she thought they were doing that moment in St. Croix. She couldn't get it out of her head.

She went to her gala meeting and was very surprised when they appointed her Co-Chair for the next year's event. They must have been impressed by her high bid the night before. The title carried a considerable amount of prestige along with the work involved to bring it all together.

That day, several more women in the group acknowledged her and started telling her about various social functions that they would like to invite her to. Susan was feeling like she was the new "darling" of the island social network. She hoped that Anthony would be by her side through all of it.

Susan survived through the evening and into the next afternoon without a call from Anthony. Her worst fears were confirmed when she saw the Palm Beach Shiny Sheet.

Again, Anthony was pictured and now looking very comfortable lying on the beach with Margit. There was a caption that read "Palm Beach Lovebirds" and it featured a spread of various cozy shots of them on their date.

Susan thought "If this date didn't mean anything to him, he was doing a great job of acting." She wanted to call up Ashley or Melanie and cry about it, but decided against it. She didn't want everyone else to know what she was going through. They would tire of it if dating Anthony continued in this manner with all its problems. She didn't want her friends to be afraid to pick up the phone.

Susan made a decision to not give him another chance to upset her. She didn't even want to hear about the date and that nothing happened. Judging by the pictures, everything was happening! It seemed effortless for Anthony to like someone. He really was just a Playboy and her heart would never be strong enough to accept that. She had to move on for her own good.

She had no plans for the evening and made a bowl of popcorn and lay on her couch watching television. She was wearing her "comfy" clothes and looked like a mess.

There was a light knock on her door. She stood up and

shuffled in her slippers to peek out the side window to see who was outside.

Anthony was there and called through the door "Susan please open up. I know you are standing there." She slowly let down on the latch and he pushed the door open. He didn't give her a chance to speak and raised her up in his arms and carried her over to the front room couch. He lay her down as he kneeled on the floor and intensely kissed her.

The copy of the newspaper was near-by on the coffee table and he reached back with his hand to pick it up. After he pulled his lips from hers, he held up the paper. "I was afraid you would see this. That "Twit" hired a photographer to follow us there. It was all staged. Look closely at them. Can't you tell I don't look happy?"

She tried to take a look, but he went in again for more kissing and Susan couldn't see or breathe. She was at one with him and did not want to stop. He was so romantic and tender. His lips were so sensuous that she felt faint.

He started talking again "We had some bad weather over there so we couldn't fly back until this afternoon. I was afraid to call you and figured that I should just come over to show you how much I care for you now. I am sorry if I made you feel bad at any time."

Susan believed him and now tried to talk but Anthony would not let her. "Susan, I want you to be my girl. I can't imagine being without you again. Please let this happen. I think we were meant to be. I have never felt like this before. Let me show you."

He picked her up from the couch and carried her up her stairs to her bedroom. They fell on the bed together and tore at each other until they both were naked.

Anthony raised his powerful thighs and began making love to her. He was filled with raw, pulsating emotion. She lay paralyzed as he consumed her. When they reached their pinnacle, he fell off her, holding her tightly and determined to never let her go.

After an hour of lying reposed and completely silent, the couple embraced again. Anthony whispered in her ear. "I am staying with you tonight. I can't bear to be without you. I love you Susan, you need to know that." Susan put her arms around him tighter and said softly "I love you too Anthony." Anthony smiled and said "You are mine forever, always know that."

CHAPTER 5

The romance between Susan and Anthony continued at a strong, unrelenting pace over the following months. He was always full of surprises and would often fly Susan off on quickie excursions to South America and the Caribbean.

They also traveled from the major European cities to the quaint chateaus in the country. Anthony spoke French and German almost as fluently as Italian. He knew his way around and had friends throughout the world. Susan had traveled to many of the same places before on her own or with her parents, but she now enjoyed seeing the world through his eyes. She never had a chance to grow tired of him. He had so much to offer.

Susan was never in doubt again that Anthony was very serious about her when he showed her his family's hometown in Sicily and introduced her to several of his relatives. He started buying her jewelry and priceless artwork. Their tastes were similar and he always delighted her.

In his spare time, they would lie out on his yacht sunning or occasionally snorkel. They had an agreement. She was only willing to get in the water if he stayed right next to her so he would get eaten first by the sharks.

He made her cut up her credit cards and he opened new accounts for her, footing all the bills. He encouraged her to buy a classier wardrobe and set her up with designers. They attended all the top parties and charity functions. Susan was proud to be seen with him. He was well-liked by everyone.

One day he surprised her with the news that they would be attending a major ball at Mar-a-Lago. It was considered to be one of the top events of the Season and was always attended by dignitaries from around the world. Susan was excited for the next three weeks awaiting the night.

Anthony paid an exorbitant amount to have her ball gown custom made by a top fashion house and rushed to her in time. It arrived the day before the ball in the late afternoon.

Susan spent the next day dressing for the party and Anthony was absolutely stunned when she paraded herself in front of him. "My God! You look like a Princess!" He smiled at her and took her arm to escort her to the white limousine waiting outside.

Susan loved everything about Mar-a-Lago, from the lion statues in front, to the magnificent paintings and furnishings! Soon after their arrival they were graciously welcomed by Donald Trump and his wife. Susan thought he looked much taller than she imagined. The gowns that were present were breathtaking and all were very unique. Nothing off the rack at this party! Everyone sparkled!

She danced with Anthony and smiled up at him with adoring eyes. He was truly her prince! He looked down at her and pulled her even closer. They were the perfect couple and it seemed that they were put on earth for each other. Susan could not imagine finding anyone else that she could be happy with. They were for keeps!

He proudly displayed her on his arm as he introduced her to various royalty and Hollywood moguls. Susan was now on a first name basis with the wealthiest people in the world and she loved this life! Even though her parents had been well-known in various circles, she now outshined them. She wished they were here to enjoy this too. She knew this was one of her mother's favorite balls. Susan was sad to see the magical night end, but her fairy tale life continued on this enchanted island.

Susan enjoyed all of Florida, and especially loved the discos of South Beach! The couple would drive down to

Miami in his different sports cars to go to the newest clubs.

Anthony was a silent partner for one of the venues and brought Susan with him on one trip to check up on the staff. It was well into the wee hours. He left her seated at a table accompanied by a large glass of wine while he went to the back office.

Susan watched the crowd dance and was quite content that she had her man and no longer needed to be part of the dating ritual. She looked around at all the excitement going on around her and saw a figure approach her through the smoky haze.

As it drew closer, the familiar face of Gregory slowly materialized. He had been dancing and sweat was soaking through the white satin shirt that clung tightly to his muscles. He came up to her and gave her a kiss on the lips. A spark went through her body and she sat up in her chair. "Susan! How nice to see you. What brings you way down to Miami?"

Susan hesitated, she still liked Gregory and did not want to ruin it by mentioning Anthony. She knew he would walk off. She avoided the question. "Gregory! You look great! How have you been?" Gregory sat down next to her, pulling his chair closer. He nuzzled her neck. Susan thought as she closed her eyes and swooned, just a bit. "He is so overpowering, I can't stop this. It is always like he has a weird hold over me."

Gregory said "Susan, I have been thinking of you quite a lot since I last saw you. Why did you disappear?" Susan laughed "You were the one that took off! Who was that woman anyway? Your wife? Was that her house that we went to?" Gregory shrugged "Does it really matter? We are here now, together once again, fate is such a sweet thing!" He moved in on her very vulnerable neck again and Susan pulled back.

****

Susan continued to have a very good month. She loved being in Palm Beach and all the culture and beauty that it offered. Her love also grew even more for Anthony. In the short slice of time since she had met him, besides the few moments of doubt, he had been nothing but perfect to her at all times. It seemed so unreal that Susan worried when a black cloud would block out it all out.

She had a special date with him tonight since it was Valentine's Day. He had just flown back from New York after an exceptionally long departure and she could hardly wait to see him. He told her that he had an extra nice gift for her.

Susan spent the day in Palm Beach Gardens looking for a dress. It was the only day she would think of wearing red. It didn't take long to find a Valentine outfit. Most of the display windows were specially set up for the day. Red was everywhere!

She kept shopping for other accessories, including four new pairs of shoes. She had wanted to shop in Boca that day too, but evening was approaching, and there was no way she would make it back in traffic on I-95 in time.

She traveled back to the island and decided to go over to one of the cafés on County Road to get some lemonade. As she walked down the sidewalk, she began feeling like someone was behind her. She turned around a few times but only saw small groups of tourists. She reached the adobe walls of the café and decided to sit on their patio.

The waitress brought her drink in a tall icy glass. Susan began slipping it slowly and debated whether to get another one with some alcohol in it. She turned her head behind her to look at an impressive sports car stopped at the corner. A man sat down quickly at her table and put a hand on her arm.

Susan turned back and was very startled. She knocked over her drink on the table. "Oh God! Oh no!" Her worst moment was happening.

Robert St. Germain was there. He picked up her glass and scooped the ice cubes back into it. He then put his cold hand on her leg, "Bet you didn't think you would see me again, did you Bitch?" Susan was scared. He looked extremely threatening, and this time there was nowhere to run off to.

He was right up in her face, keeping his voice low. "You know I went to jail for two years because of you! You thought I would never find out that you were behind everything?" He kept a tight grip on her arm.

Susan looked around frantically and saw they were they only ones in the patio section. She insisted "I don't know what you're talking about!" He painfully pushed down on her arm. Susan sharply said "You screwed *me* over! You owe me money, a lot of money!" She bravely shook her arm from his hand saying "You know Robert, there are a lot of people looking for you across the country! Why do you think I did anything?"

Robert got even madder "Don't even try to get out of this! I know it was you. But I can't figure how you set it all up? Either way, I am going to remove you from this planet! You have to go!" Susan was scared, but calmly said "You are a paranoid psycho and you know it." She knew he was just throwing things out there.

Luckily for Susan, the waitress came back out and gave St. Germain a curious look. Susan said "Can I have my check please?" The waitress started to walk off to get it

It was almost time for her date with Anthony. Her hand was shaking as she tried to put on her make-up. She was very scared that she saw St. Germain and she debated whether to tell her boyfriend.

As the sun began to settle down, Anthony arrived. She was relieved to see him and instantly felt better. He gave her a bouquet of red roses and held her for a long time. Susan put the flowers in a vase by her front door. Anthony had his red Lamborghini with him for the occasion and he drove her over to an intimate restaurant on the island.

Romance was in the air and there were roses on all the tables. Susan wondered which table would be for them. Instead, of waiting to be seated, Anthony led her out of the main dining room and onto the terrace.

There was a single table out there set up just for them. Soft classical music was playing and it was beautiful under the stars. Their only light was a single candle. Susan watched as the shadows flickered across Anthony's handsome face as he sat across from her.

They began their meal with red wine. He held up his glass to her and said "Here's to my dream girl. Happy Valentine's Day!" She toasted him back smiling. He leaned over the table and gave her a kiss.

Anthony then rose up and walked over to her. He got down on one knee and pulled a black velvet box from his pocket. He opened it up with his thumb while presenting it to her.

"Susan, I have only known you for a short time. But, I want to spend the rest of our time as your husband. I love you, will you please marry me?"

Susan was enchanted! "Of course I will marry you Anthony! I love you too!" He slid the ring onto her finger. It was breathtaking and sparkled in the candlelight. Susan was absolutely touched and delighted! She didn't know that this was the gift he was talking about.

Anthony rose back up and pulled his chair right next to her. They kissed for a long time. His lips were so sweet and she felt like she now officially belonged to him.

Anthony grinned "I wanted to do this after dinner, but the time was perfect and I didn't want to wait!" Susan said excitedly "I don't know if I can eat now, I'm all butterflies!" He smiled, "Now, for your gift, we might as well get that out of the way now too!" Susan said "There's more?"

They walked out a side gate. There, in front of the restaurant, was a white Ferrari convertible with a wide red bow wrapped around it. Susan ran up to it. A single white rose lay on the front seat. Anthony kissed her on the cheek and said "Happy Valentine's Honey!"

Susan said "Now I'm definitely not going to be able to eat! I want to drive it!" Anthony pulled on her arm "Come on. Let's go back. I want to tell you about our honeymoon!"

She reluctantly and happily returned to sit at the table. Anthony had already ordered for them and the waiter arrived with lobster. Susan squealed "Oh goody, this is just what I wanted to eat!" Anthony asked her "Would you like to get married in April, right before the end of Season?"

She looked puzzled "This April? That soon?" Anthony said sweetly "I was hoping you wanted to do it this year too."

Susan thought about it and then assured him, "I would love to get married right away! Are we eloping?" Anthony replied "No, no, we are going to have a fabulous wedding. I know it takes time to plan, but I have all the connections to make sure that everything you want to do for it can be taken care of right away!"

She took his hand. "If that can happen, then let's do it!" Anthony then asked her slowly "And where is your favorite place for a honeymoon?" Susan gleefully said "Bora, Bora!"

He smiled and reached over and hugged her. "That's what I thought you would say! That's my dream place too! I have never been there. We're going! I booked it!" Susan cooed "Going to Bora Bora in the spring is the best time to do it! It's all perfect!"

They decided to get married early in April, two weeks after Easter. Season would still be happening on their wedding day and many of their guests, which were mainly his friends and associates, would still be in the area. Susan said "Wow, I need to start calling my girlfriends tonight! Hope they can all make it!"

They enjoyed the rest of their dinner. Susan kept holding up her ring and admired it. After they finished their dessert, they jumped into her Ferrari and took off for the ocean.

Anthony and Susan held hands walking down the sidewalk along Ocean Drive. Susan wanted to walk in the sand, but didn't want it ruining her new car, so she changed her mind.

As they walked slowly, they talked about having kids. They both wanted them right away. Anthony said "Christ, we aren't getting any younger! Let's start making them tonight! I have a reservation for us at The Breakers!" Susan wedged up right next to him as they went back to the car. She wanted him to drive. He kept his arm around her as they motored back to the restaurant. Anthony wasn't about to leave his Lamborghini on the street overnight, so they drove their cars side by side and smiled at each other on the way to the resort.

Anthony and his fiancée shared a beautiful and romantic night. He arranged to have some of their clothes delivered to them, so after breakfast, they went on the golf course for a quick nine holes. Before Anthony let Susan go back to her Ferrari, he held her and twirled her around saying "I want you to move into my house with me." Susan was hesitant "I'll live with you, but I'm not selling my house until after we're married."

Anthony looked a bit defeated "I am going to buy you a mansion on the ocean, just like I know you want!" Susan chuckled "Well, if you are going to do that, then I would probably try to start selling it now. But I won't close the deal until after the honeymoon!" She loved the fact they were planning a life together. She had been on her own for too long!

Anthony looked at his Rolex and said "I would love to reserve the Breakers for another night, but I need to go home to New York to help my brothers handle some issues. I don't know how long it is going to take, but I'll call you every night and put you to bed."

Susan pouted "Can't I come with?" He answered "No, I want you here. You can start moving your stuff in and I will have my House Manager make all your arrangements." Susan said reluctantly "OK, I guess. I am going to miss you!"

Anthony said firmly "I want you to stay out of the clubs! Look at your ring every time you think about going out. You're mine now! Stay home, and start knitting some baby booties." She looked at him like he was joking. He was smiling, but she couldn't be sure. "I'm going to impregnate you next time I see you. So stop taking the pill." Susan laughed "Not until we're married. We are doing this the right way!"

CHAPTER 6

It was late March and the wedding now appeared on the horizon. Susan was head over heels in love with her fiancé, but was getting nervous. She was a little apprehensive about actually going through with it. To do this meant total responsibility and commitment. It was not an easy thing for her to say "I will love you forever," especially since she was still young.

Susan thought "It must be a full moon coming up if I am thinking like this!" Anthony was in New York again and she was lonely. She decided to cheer up and go to a lounge on the island that night. Melanie was in town from California, so she called her up and arranged to meet her inside one of the Breaker's bars after 9 PM. Susan was feeling a little dark and searched through her closet for a nasty, but appropriate "little black dress."

She decided on a leopard print and to wear her hair down tonight. She sat at her dressing table and sipped on a Chocolate Martini. She spent about fifteen minutes straightening her hair completely flat. She viewed herself in the mirror and was surprised that she looked like she was in her early twenties again. Susan then worried and thought that maybe she should try a different look in case she ran into any Fiore acquaintances. "What the heck! I only have less than a month left to party!" She assumed Melanie was dressing to kill and she had to outdo her!

She valeted Anthony's Black Ferrari and slowly walked into the hotel. She found Melanie sitting at the bar talking with a gentleman from Canada. The bartender also seemed interested in her and was leaning on the bar with his elbows, trying to join in the conversation.

Susan sat down next to her. She ordered wine and

observed the people. The bar was half-filled and just some of the tables were occupied. Susan thought that there must be a major party going on somewhere else. The rest of the crowd would probably show up later towards closing.

CHAPTER 7

April was approaching and Susan was sitting by the pool at Anthony's. As usual, she was alone minding the fort. She didn't care about his trips anymore and actually relished this time by herself to take care of all the final wedding preparations.

Lately, her fiancé had been going out of his way to make sure that she knew how much he loved her. All of the bumps were now smoothed out and she was ready to take on a life with him. He finally figured out how Susan ticked and all the right things to say to her. They loved each other very much and she now accepted that it was a lasting love and that she was mature enough to handle it.

Anthony made good on his promise that Susan could have the greatest wedding that Palm Beach had ever seen. He truly acted like he wanted to make all her dreams come true. The fact that he had modified his own life so that she could live in Palm Beach full-time and have her dream oceanfront mansion, attested to this.

It was not easy, but Anthony was able to book a church on the island at the last minute. It had been close to impossible to achieve this! Susan had always wanted to marry there ever since she was a child and first fell in love with the town.

She was very excited about her guest list. Almost everyone had already been invited and there were only a few declines. Anthony said she could fly her favorites in on his private jet.

There were also some acquaintances that she had sent an invitation to in order to just rub their noses in it, but she hoped they wouldn't actually accept. She was also making sure that their wedding announcement would appear in the newspapers of all the major cities. How exciting!

She began thinking of her childhood friends that she could

invite at the last minute. The first person that came to mind was Michael Hansen. It had been a while since Susan saw him at the dinner show. She assumed that he was still living near the North Shore and thought it would be great to have him there!

It was pretty easy to find him. She logged into FaceBook and he was on there! She looked at his Friend's list and saw a lot of familiar names. She then looked at his photos. There were many pictures of him at sporting events and posing with different girls. She made more inquiries and came up with his current and past addresses, and the companies he had worked for. Seems that he was now the Chief Financial Officer for a global manufacturer that was headquartered in Chicago. She still didn't see any mention about a wife anywhere. Good! Still single! She wondered if he knew his personal cell phone number was out there for all to see. It probably was long disconnected. She decided to try it anyway.

She dialed the number and it immediately went to voice mail. She waited a minute and tried again. This time it rang. Susan became very nervous and wasn't sure what she would say if this was still Michael's number.

CHAPTER 8

When Susan woke up the next morning, a rose from the garden was lying on the pillow next to her. Anthony left her a note that he had to leave town again for business. It did not say where he was going. She figured it was New York again and thought "Was he insane? He's never going to have time to get ready for the wedding on Saturday!"

Susan was overwhelmed, there was just too much to do. Some of the guests would be arriving from out of town tomorrow. She took her pillow, covered her head and went back for more sleep. She was awakened a few hours later when she heard knocking on the front door.

She looked out the bedroom window and all she could see was the head of a tall man that was standing below. She quickly brushed her hair back and dressed in a summer cocktail dress. She felt a sense of excitement and ran down the stairs barefoot. She thought she had an idea who it was and glanced nervously at the mirror to the side of the door. All was good. Susan closed her eyes and slowly turned the door handle.

She then opened them wide and was now looking through the eyes of a sixteen year old. It was Michael! She felt like she couldn't breathe when she saw him standing there and smiling at her.

He reached out for her, taking both her hands. She felt faint as he slowly pulled her into his arms for a light embrace. He quietly said "It is so wonderful to see you again. So, you're getting married in a few days! How exciting is that?" Susan beckoned to them, "Come on into the house!" Michael looked at the exterior and the imported hand-sculpted Italian statues near the door. He kept nodding his head "Wow, this is pretty impressive." He followed Susan into the kitchen. She opened the refrigerator and handed him a Heineken. Michael sipped at his beer and apologized to her for his surprise visit. "My cell phone signal isn't strong enough here. I couldn't get in a call to you. I came a day early to work on my tan so I can wear shorts again. It is still pretty cold back at home." He stuck out his arm. "I'm pasty!"

She gave him a big smile. "Well, I am very glad to see you. Every time I ran into you I never had the chance to get a good look at you." She laughed, "You seemed to have ripened very nicely!" He was still very muscular and even more handsome. His blue eyes were so trusting and sweet. They both gazed at each other. Michael came closer to her and Susan felt her heart pounding against her chest!

The phone in Anthony's study suddenly rang. Susan looked in that direction and said "I am sorry Michael, I have to go see who that is." She was gone for five minutes. When she came back she looked apologetic and said "I am sorry to cut this visit short Michael. That was Anthony and he needs me to go into town and do some bank business for him right away. Is it ok if you stop by again later this week? Maybe you can meet him them. I forgot to tell him you were here."

Michael quickly replied "Of course, Susan! I need to get over to a golf game I set up anyway. I will give you a call!" He then lightly brushed her cheek with a kiss and went out to his rental car. Susan smiled as she watched him walk down the driveway. She was sad to see him go.

The wedding week flew by. Just one more day! All the guests started trickling into town. The rehearsal dinner was coming up in a few hours and Anthony was still not back from New York yet with his two brothers. His sisters and mother had already called and left a message that they were poolside at The Colony with a pitcher of Margaritas and a bunch of cousins. Susan was thinking of joining them, but still had too many things to do, and alcohol wouldn't help with that. It was nice that Anthony had so many relatives.

Susan's sisters were not coming because they were off on a trip to South Africa together with their husbands. They were a bit annoyed that Susan didn't plan her wedding more in advance. Susan didn't even worry about her brother John, she had no clue where he was since she saw him on the island, and she didn't really care. He knew she was getting married and made no attempt to contact her about it. She had no other immediate relatives. Her Godfather, who now lived in Naples, and well into his eighties, would be walking her down the aisle.

It was Susan's best girlfriends that were her real family. Her three bridesmaids and Ashley, who was her Maid of Honor, were ready to go. Melanie and Linda were also flying in from the West Coast.

Susan spent the rest of the day in meetings with her make-up and hair stylist. Anthony finally called her from the airport and said that they had just landed and that he would see her over at the rehearsal. He was headed over to The Colony first to meet up with his relatives. Susan said she would pop over as soon as she was able.

She made one more call before getting ready. It was to Michael. He was still over at his hotel and had just finished playing tennis. He was walking off the courts when he answered her call. Susan was pacing her living room and straightening it up while half-holding her cell to her ear.

"Michael, I hope you are enjoying the island. I am sorry I haven't had the time to get back to you. It doesn't look like there is going to be anytime to meet Anthony. He just flew back into town and we have to go to our rehearsal soon."

Michael laughed "Don't worry Susan, I know you are probably overwhelmed." Susan was happy that he was so understanding. He then said "I am going to come over and see you today because I know you will be too busy for good-byes tomorrow. I need to talk to you. Are you going to be at the house?" Susan replied "Yes, for a little while, so please come by now. Then I have to get over to the church. I will see you soon. Bye!" She put down the phone and was excited about seeing him again. She was glad they could be alone.

She waited for him out on the front walk. A half-hour later, the rental pulled up. Michael pulled his 6'3 foot frame out of the tiny sports car. He looked fantastic and was fully dressed in a dark business suit. He was carrying a bouquet of exotic flowers and walked up to her, then kneeled down to present them to her.

He bowed his head and said "Only the best for such an exquisite woman." He rose and placed them into her hands. Susan giggled. "Thank you, sir! How lovely." He gave her a kiss on the cheek, his cologne was heavenly.

Michael looked around and immediately asked "Is Tony here?" Susan said "No. He is meeting me at the rehearsal. He is busy rounding up his family." Michael looked relieved "Great! Can we drive over to the beach?" Susan said "That will be nice."

He opened the door of the car for her and held her hand to guide her in. As he got in next to her, Michael gave a long look into her eyes. Susan gazed back at him for a moment, and then cocked her head curiously, before pulling her eyes away. She was starting to feel a little warm.

He started the car up, drove past the beach that was by the house, and kept going. Susan watched the side of his face and thought about how chiseled his profile looked. He kept driving until he reached a magnificent stretch of road overlooking the finest views of the ocean that Palm Beach had to offer.

He backed the car into a parking spot across the street. With the excitement of a child, Susan asked "Do you want to walk along the shore? We can't access any beach here." She pointed "I know of a little pathway off the side down there." Michael said "I'm game" and stood up outside the car taking off his suit coat. He reached down and untied his shoes. Susan got out and walked around the hood. She put a hand on his back while she steadied herself removing her sandals. Walking carefully over the hot cement, Michael helped her down a small incline which led to a very narrow, but long strip of sand.

When they got back in the car, it was like leaving a time tunnel. Susan pulled her hand back from his and started looking at her nails to see if her polish chipped. Michael turned to her smiling and said "Well...?" Susan seemed withdrawn.

She was now obviously back in the present with a myriad of responsibilities facing her and her love for Anthony still intact. She cut him off, "Honestly, Michael, I think that all this has ever been about was that "ancient kiss" looking for a resolution." Businesslike, she wiped some more sand off her neck. "You should have looked for me sooner and maybe if that had happened, things could have been different. I really need to get over to the rehearsal."

She looked down at the door handle. She knew she was avoiding some heartfelt issues, because Susan did feel strongly for Michael. But she couldn't let him know it or he would stop her plans. Even though Anthony seemed to be distant at times and more interested in being in New York, he was still the one she wanted unless something else changed everything. She couldn't sabotage her life any longer for a moment that couldn't easily define its outcome.

Without saying anything more to him, Michael understood what she was thinking. He pulled out of the parking lot and headed back to Anthony's to deliver his bride.

Susan was running late and rummaged through her closet to grab her special dress that she was wearing to the rehearsal and dinner. She was very upset that the water wrecked her hair. There was no time to get a hair dresser over there. She was tempted to go look for an old wig she had for just this reason, but feared it was in an unmarked box somewhere. She heavily moussed her ends and holding her head upside down, she voraciously blew it with a dryer as she saturated it with styling spray. The results made her look a bit wild and rough around the edges, instead of the sophisticated look that her dress called for.

Anthony had arranged for a limousine to pick her up. She had just finished slapping on her make-up when the driver pulled up and called on her cell. She hurriedly applied her lipstick as she went out to the driveway.

As they made their way along the ocean, the water was darkening and Susan turned to her right to see the sun setting to the west over the treetops. It was a beautiful night. She calmed down a bit and was looking forward to meeting everyone. She was especially anxious to see Anthony again.

The church was dark, but the altar area was lit up. Anthony had a special agreement with the priest to enable them to come there this late instead of the afternoon. All of the wedding party was standing up there watching the door. As Susan walked through it, they looked relieved. Anthony walked down the aisle with a frown on his face to greet her. He gave her a quick and worried kiss on her forehead.

Pulling hard on her arm, he said "You look like you're ready to hit the clubs. What's with the hair?" Susan felt a bit annoyed "I had some disasters trying to get ready." Anthony snapped, "I really need you to make a good impression. My family doesn't think I've known you long enough." Susan was wondering where this nasty attitude came from. She teared up a bit and just looked steadfastly ahead. She then took her first look at his three sisters standing in the front. She couldn't help but be amused and thought, "He's worried about what I look like?"

CHAPTER 9

In another part of the hotel, Susan began preparing for her ceremony. She knew Michael was staying in the same place and she didn't dare try to contact him since she was uneasy that Anthony might actually be keeping spies on her. Susan badly wanted to ask Michael's advice, and what he thought about the Mafia claims that Antonia made. Even more, she desperately wanted him to tell her again how much he had always cared for her. She also wanted to hear him say that it was a big mistake that she was getting married to Anthony! She really needed this, she couldn't think for herself anymore! It was all closing in on her! Anthony had acted terribly the night before and she was no longer convinced that she wanted to be with him. Her impassioned moment with Michael wouldn't let her.

Susan took a long shower and tried not to think at all. She placed a towel on her head and waited for her hair stylist. She was surprised that Anthony hadn't called her yet. Susan drummed her fingers nervously on the wooden coffee table as she glanced at the television. She heard a knock. The stylist arrived right on time. Susan now devoted herself to getting ready, but felt like she was just going through the motions, because her heart was not into it.

Michael lay on his hotel bed and felt like a kicked dog. He was depressed that Susan was almost his yesterday and then he lost her to cold reality. He groaned in pain as he rolled off the bed and headed to the closet. The wedding was now an hour away, but he wasn't sure if he should still go since Susan didn't mention it either way when he left her at the beach. It was too much to see her marry that jerk!

But, he thought of her happiness and that she would value his blessing, so he decided to attend. Michael had an imported Italian suit that he knew would outrank the groom. As he was trying to find a tie in his suitcase, he thought about the men that beat him up. It was a sure bet that they were friends of Tony, or maybe they were his mobbed up brothers. He was worried. If Tony Fiore was gunning for you it wasn't good news!

He thought about grabbing some food first and then realized where he was and yelled in exasperation "There's no McDonald's on this God forsaken island! This day completely sucks!" He just wanted to go rent a jet ski and get lost in the ocean somewhere."

Michael reluctantly finished dressing and left his room. He was very worried about Susan. She had no clue what Fiore was about and what she was getting herself into. And, he was afraid to do anything about it because he would probably get himself killed. But, Michael still couldn't help thinking that this was something she could not handle by herself.

On the floor below, Susan had finished having her make-up done and her hair styled with small flowers to make her look like a goddess. She waited patiently until her bridesmaids arrived. Ashley showed up first and looked sheepish as Susan greeted her. She had recovered from her drunken tryst with Marco, was forgiven, and was handed the garment bag containing the wedding dress.

The group walked into the hallway. Each woman was carrying an array of accessories to bring to the church and finish dressing there. The bridal party reached the first floor and headed to the white Rolls Royce awaiting them outside. Unfortunately for him, Michael's elevator arrived just after the girls.

in a few minutes. Laughing and sipping champagne, they helped Susan dress. Finally, when she was as perfect as she could look, the maids left to go take their places.

Susan sat for a while at the dressing table and studied herself. She looked radiant! But she didn't look happy. She tried to laugh when she caught herself looking up at the small window above her. It was the only way out! She thought "Might be a tight fit in this dress!"

Her heart was now a hard pit in her stomach. She closed her eyes and envisioned Michael and her on the rock. *The water was peaceful. They were now making love.* She needed to be with him.

THE END

www.ingramcontent.com/pod-product-compliance
Lightning Source LLC
Chambersburg PA
CBHW072358030726
47505CB00014B/1889